Oh Deer!

BRANDI SMELTZER

Illustrations by Mau Rendón

Green Meadow Publishing

Cover design and illustrations by Mau Rendón
Hardback ISBN: 978-1-7345738-0-0
Paperback ISBN: 978-1-7345738-1-7

Library of Congress Control Number: 2020904893

Smeltzer, Brandi
Oh Deer! / Brandi Smeltzer
As a thunderstorm looms in the distance, seven-year-old Brooklyn spots a young animal in trouble.
Brooklyn must decide whether to intervene or allow nature to run its course.
Based on a true story.

ISBN: 978-1-7345738-1-7

For Brooklyn, Brinden, and Haylen, who are always willing to help those in need—and for Doug, without whom this book would not have been possible.

Thank you to my editors Alexis, Lael, and Marcy. You girls are awesome!

Brooklyn stood at her living room window, peering across the backyard to the gray sky over the neighboring wheat field.

Nearing harvest, the golden crop swayed in the misty breeze. A storm was coming. She didn't like storms.

The thunder always made her tremble.

Brooklyn examined the dark clouds looming in the distance when movement near the fence line caught her eye.

A flash of brown, just slightly darker than the wheat, charged at the woven wire.

"There's something out there
trying to get through the fence!"
she said to her parents.

But what was it?

The distance made it hard to tell.

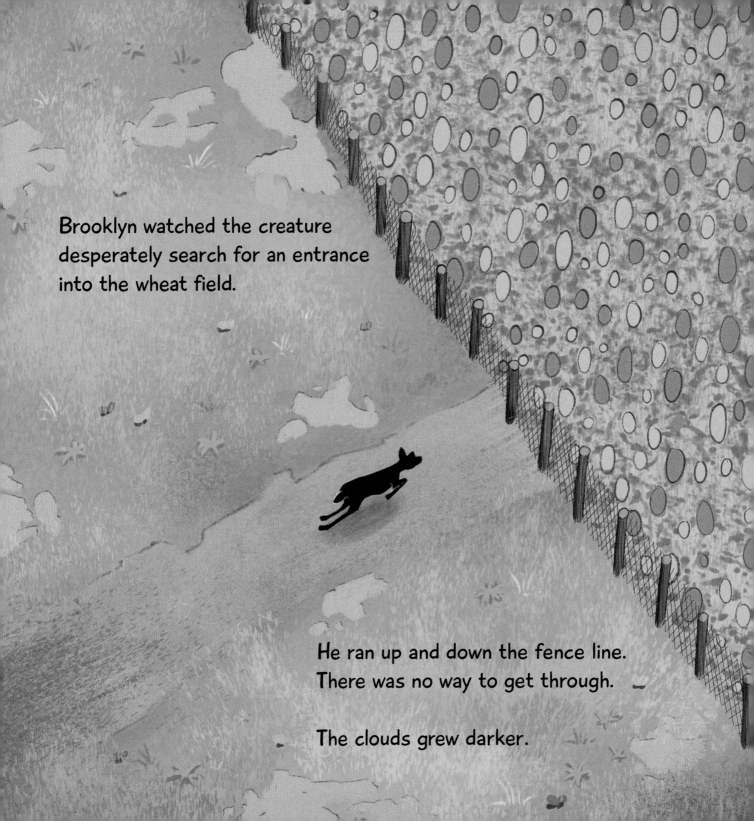

Brooklyn watched the creature desperately search for an entrance into the wheat field.

He ran up and down the fence line. There was no way to get through.

The clouds grew darker.

Then the animal turned from the fence and ran in the direction of Brooklyn's house. She could see it clearly now. "It's a little deer!" she cried.

"And he's

LOST!"

The white-tailed fawn reversed its direction and darted back toward the fence, preparing to jump.

He stopped right in front of the wire, too afraid to take the leap.

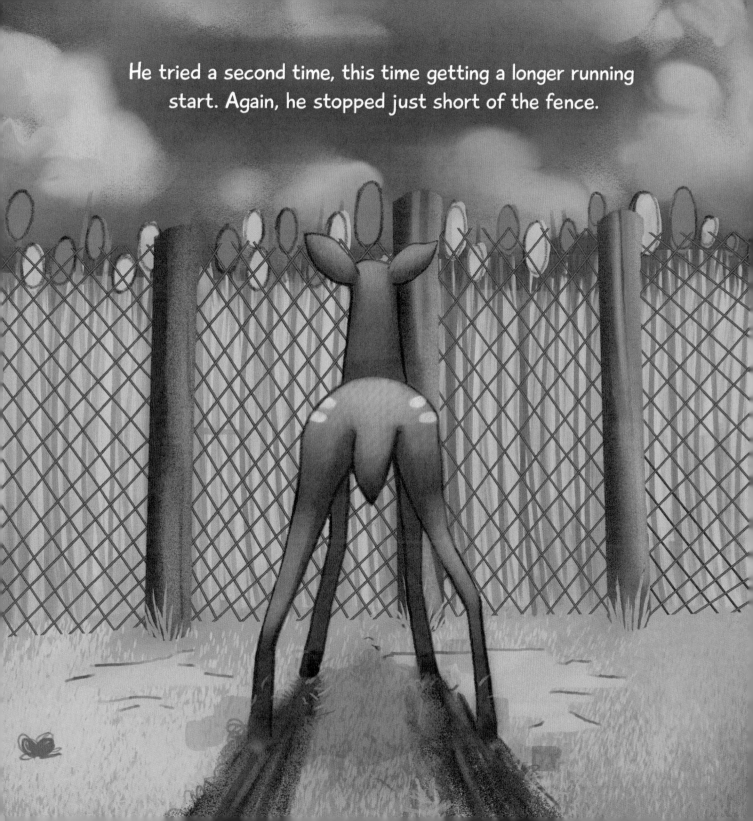

He tried a second time, this time getting a longer running start. Again, he stopped just short of the fence.

His small legs were not yet strong enough to make the five-foot jump.

"COME ON, LITTLE DEER, YOU CAN DO IT!" Brooklyn cheered.

The tree branches swayed wildly.

He made several more attempts, coming increasingly nearer to Brooklyn's house each time.

At one point, he even approached the window, his eyes wide with fear.

Brooklyn could see white spots on his back near his tail.

"HE'S JUST A BABY!"

she cried to her parents.

The clouds rolled in much faster now, and the first streak of lightning flashed across the sky.

"How can a fawn this young survive the storm alone? **WE HAVE TO HELP HIM!**"

Fortunately, Brooklyn's father knew that deer often leave their fawns.

"I know you want to help," he told her,

"but his mommy is nearby, and if we go out there, we might scare her away. We need to leave the fawn exactly where he is so the mother can come back to him."

"But I don't see her," Brooklyn bellowed.
Thunder rumbled overhead like a stampede of elephants.
She panicked.

"WE HAVE TO DO SOMETHING!"

Brooklyn could see something swiveling right above the wheat's surface.
An ear!

"THERE SHE IS!"

Brooklyn said with excitement.

"THE BABY'S MOTHER!"

The fawn wasn't lost after all.

The mother was right there all along,
watching over her young.

"I'm glad we didn't try to help," Brooklyn said. "We might have scared her away from her baby. Then he really *would* have been alone in the storm."

Just then, the doe's body rose from the wheat
as she leaped over the fence and landed beside
her fawn. Brooklyn breathed a sigh of relief.

She could see that the fawn was now in the safety of his mother's care.

Together, mother and baby
ran toward the nearby wood.

Brooklyn watched their white tails rise and fall
as they disappeared into the shelter of the trees.

As lightning flashed in the west, Brooklyn's mother guided her away from the window.

Brooklyn knew that, like the fawn, she was in the safety of her own mother's care.

WHAT TO DO IF YOU SPOT A FAWN ALL ALONE

Brooklyn is not the first to experience this dilemma. Spotting a fawn without its mother is a common experience, and many well-meaning citizens react just like Brooklyn; they want to help. But their attempt to help the young deer may do more harm than good.

What many people do not realize is that mother deer normally leave their young alone for long stretches of time—sometimes up to six hours! But do not be fooled; when Mom leaves, she does not go far. Her large, cup-shaped ears provide her with a keen sense of hearing, and she swivels them so that she can hear in any direction. This helps her keep track of her fawn. If he needs her, he will cry out, and she will return to him. However, if mommy deer is eating and does not sense any danger, she may wait a while before returning. It is crucial that she stays well fed so she can provide milk for her baby.

If humans try to help, they may leave a scent on the baby that could attract predators. Additionally, removing a fawn from its location could result in the permanent separation of mother and baby. Experts say that it is best to leave the fawn alone, intervening only if it is certain that the fawn has been orphaned or has been on its own for more than 12 hours.

FUN FACTS

White-tailed deer spend most of their lives in one specific area known as their home range.

A female deer's home range covers about one square mile.

Mother deer make their nests on the forest floor.

White-tailed fawns are born in the spring and lose their spots by late October.

A fawn's spots help it blend in with plants while its mother is finding food.

Newborn fawns have little scent, so predators do not find them easily.

Mother deer leave their fawns alone much of the day, returning several times to nurse.

At three weeks, fawns are old enough to follow their mothers on outings away from the nest.

Fawns stay with their mothers for about one year.

ABOUT THE AUTHOR

Brandi Smeltzer is a former middle school language arts teacher who left public education to homeschool her three children. She enjoys reading, writing, and spending quality time with her family. Brandi lives in Indiana with her husband and three children.

To learn more information, visit http://BrandiSmeltzer.com.

ABOUT THE ILLUSTRATOR

Mauricio "Mau" Rendón has lived all his life in Mexico City. He is passionate about animation, video games, and board games. He also enjoys spending time with his family and his pit bull Bosco.

Made in the USA
Las Vegas, NV
28 December 2024

15475561R00021